WHAT DID I GET MYSELF INTO?

I CAN'T SEE JACK SHIT.
MAYBE.
UH, MAYBE THIS WAS ASKING TOO MUCH?

AND THESE CUFFS...
DEFINITELY
SHOULD HAVE
GOTTEN A DIFFERENT
COLOR.
RAINBOW WAS
A POOR CHOICE.
BUH
BUMP
I DIDN'T KNOW
WHAT I WAS DOING
SHOPPING ALL BY
MYSELF.

TIC TAC
TIC
TAC

HMM?

SPECIAL DELIVERY!
POP
HUH?
DID I MISS ANOTHER HOLIDAY?

WHAT? NO!
YOU DON'T NEED A HOLIDAY FOR GIFTS.
ESPECIALLY A GIFT FOR MY AWESOME, HARDWORKING WIFE!

SURPRISES OBSERVE NO DATES, RIGHT?
RIGHT BEN! YOU'RE THE BEST!
DON'T IMITATE ME.

SORRY!
SORRY.

I KNOW YOU'VE HAD A LONG DAY.
BUT OPEN IT!

YOU SHOULD TAKE A BREAK!
YOU'LL LOVE IT.
I PROMISE.

IT'S REALLY COOL!

PLEAAAASE?

...

PAT PAT

SIGH
I GUESS I COULD.

I HAVE BEEN
WORKING ALL DAY.
SWEET!

SO.
WHAT DID YOU GET ME?
NOT EVEN A HINT?
OPEN IT.
NOPE! JUST OPEN IT.
OK! GIMME A SEC.
YOU'RE SO EXCITED.
IT MUST BE REALLY COO-
...
...
THIS.
UH. ISN'T FOR ME. IS IT?

JUST BUY HER SOMETHING.
A PRESENT.
IT'LL BE FUN!
BLEGH
TAP
TAP
TAP
I DIDN'T THINK I'D BE SO NERVOUS.
BEING BLINDFOLDED AND CUFFED FOR THE FIRST TIME IS WEIRD.
I CAN STILL USE MY LEGS.
MAYBE I CAN-
SHUFFLE
WIGGLE
WOBBLE
N-NO.
PLAT!
THAT WON'T END WELL.
MY GOD.
WHERE IS SHE?
WHY IS SHE MAKING ME WAIT LIKE THIS?
THE SILENCE IS KILLING ME.

WHAT ARE YOU TALKING ABOUT?!
OF COURSE THEY'RE FOR YOU!
SEE! I GOT RAINBOWS.
SO PRETTY!
AND-
RUMMAGE

LOOK! ONE OF THOSE WEIRD DICKS.
WITH THE GOLF BALL SHAPE.

IT'S NOT CALLED THAT BUT-
ALSO...!
CUTE CLOTHES.
YOU LOVE PURPLE!
Corset Co...
Size Petite
Includes:
Corset
...ties
...ockings
...ells
...histles
LOTS OF OTHER STUFF IN HERE TOO.
HERE.
FLUFF!
CRASH
LEMME JUST DUMP IT.

THEY SUGGESTED SO MUCH. I COULDN'T CHOOSE!
I GUESS I GOT A BIT CARRIED AWAY.
I WAS EXCITED. FOR US!
COOL GIFT, RIGHT?
WAG
WAG

...
...

SNRK
DO YOU-
BAE BUTTER
WATER BASED LUBE
NO PAIN
NO GAIN
NO WAY!
THAT'S OUR MOTTO
SLIDE GLIDE & CANONBALL IN.
THIS WATER-BASED LUBE PROVIDES EASY BACKDOOR ACCESS & 'PLAYS NICE' WITH TOYS.
NOTHING IS TOO BIG IN OUR BOOK. THAT SHOULD GO DOUBLE FOR YOU!
-WANT ME TO USE THESE ON YOU?

EH?
UH.

I-
UH-

YES, KINDA. I REALLY LIKE WHAT WE DID LAST TIME.
I THOUGHT MAYBE-
I MEAN.
I THINK IT'S REALLY HOT WHEN YOU'RE DOMINANT.
I WANTED TO TRY MORE.
DUDE!

DON'T BE NERVOUS!
I'M SO COOL WITH THIS!

I LOVE YOU!

BESIDES. I'VE DONE WEIRDER STUFF THAN THIS!
WAIT. WHAT STUFF?

JUST GOTTA CLIP THIS HERE.
NOW STRAP THIS. ALMOST-
SWEET, IT FITS!
HOURS (5 MINUTES) LATER
OK! I'LL BE RIGHT BACK.
...
CALM DOWN.
SHE'S JUST GETTING READY.
STEADY.
SHE SEEMED INTO IT. I HOPE-
I'VE SEEN PORN. LOTS OF PORN BUT-
I'M JUST USED TO TOPPING SO-A-AH.
FUCK. DON'T GET TOO EXCITED.
I CAN'T WAIT ANY LONGER-
WHERE'S MY WIFE?!
OVER HERE, FLUFFBUTT.

...

WHAT?

OH. RIGHT. YOU CAN'T.

THERE WE GO!
NOW-

LIKE WHAT YOU SEE?

THE
BIG
REVEAL!
TURN
YES, I DIDN'T FUCK THE SIZES UP!

SORRY FOR THE WAIT.
THIS WAS HARD TO PUT ON.
I SHOULD HAVE ASKED FOR HELP.
♥NUZZLE♥
AH!
YOU'RE WEARING THE THING!
THE THING I PICKED OUT!
I LOVE IT.
MAYBE WE SHOULDN'T COVER MY EYES.

SHH! IT'LL RUIN THE EXPERIENCE!
I PROMISE IT WILL BE FUN!
LICK
HEY.
YOU'RE NOT GONNA MAKE ME DO ANYTHING CRAZY-
-ARE YOU?
OH, HAHA.

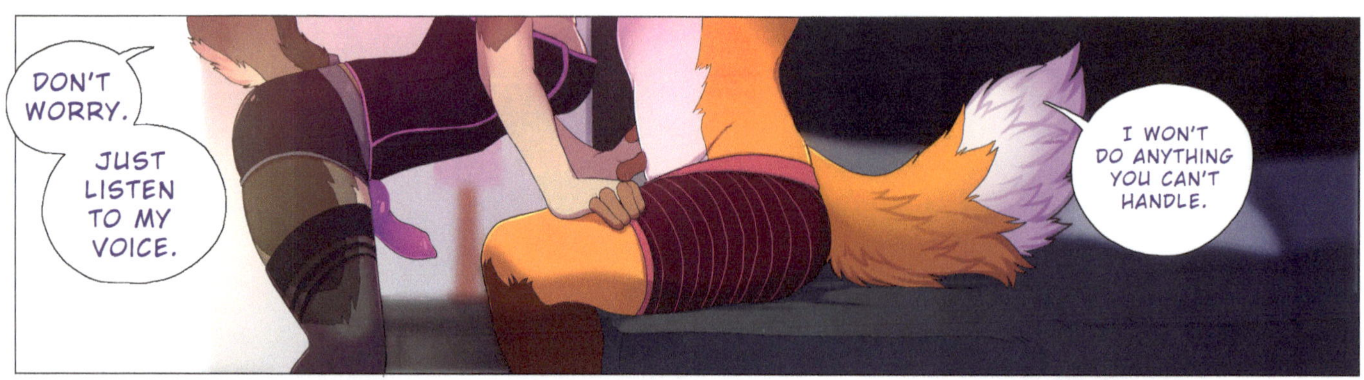
DON'T WORRY.
JUST LISTEN TO MY VOICE.
I WON'T DO ANYTHING YOU CAN'T HANDLE.
AND WHAT IF-
- I CAN'T?
THAT'S WHY WE HAVE A SAFEWORD!
SPIDERS

TILT
WHY ARE YOU WHISPERING?
SPIDERS

MY GOD!
THERE ARE SPIDERS?
YOU TRICKED ME!
THIS WAS ALL A DIRTY TRICK!
THAT'S THE SAFEWORD! JEEZE.
THEY'RE NOT SUPPOSED TO BE SEXY!
YOU NERD.
HEY! I'M NOT A NERD.

QUIET.
I WILL CALL YOU WHATEVER I WANT.
AND
YOU WILL ANSWER ME.
MH!

READY?
Y-YEAH...
I SAID-

READY?
AH! YES!
GOT IT?
CLIP
TUG
YOU WILL CALL ME SIR FROM NOW ON.
YES SIR!

YOU'RE MY PET.
I KNOW YOU'LL BE A GOOD BOY.
NICE AND OBEDIENT.
AND I HAVE A LOT PLANNED FOR YOU.
OFF THE BED!
DOWN ON YOUR KNEES!
GOOD DOG.
NOW—
LICK IT.

WHAT'S WRONG?
LET'S NOT BE SHY!
DON'T TELL ME THIS THE FIRST DICK YOU'VE EVER SUCKED?
IT IS THOUGH.
WELL.
GET TO IT THEN.
SMOOSH
NICE
AH
AND
LICK
SLOW
GOOD BOY!
mmhhh

HOW DOES
IT TASTE?

LOOKS
TO ME

LIKE
YOU'RE
ENJOYING
YOUR FIRST
TIME.

THERE
YOU GO.

A BIT
DEEPER.

THAT'A
BOY.

PRESS
UP
AGAINST THAT
KNOT.

PERFECT.

NOW...

ENOUGH
DAYDREAMING!

TAKE IT ALL.
CHU

THE
WHOLE
SLURP

THING.
MMH

YAWN

HM.
THAT'S A LITTLE BIT...

TOO SLOW.

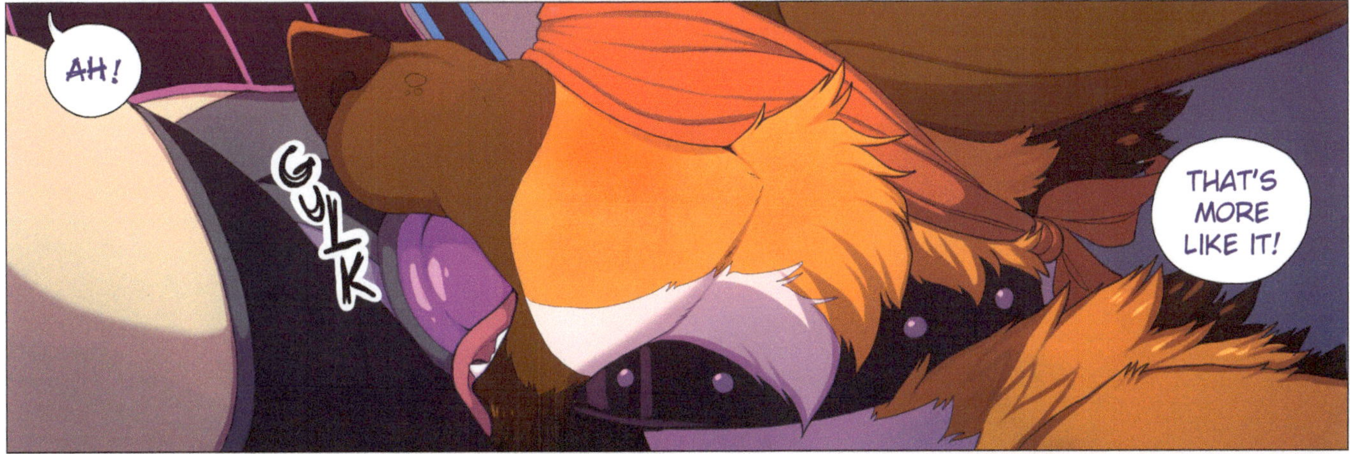

AH!
GULK
THAT'S MORE LIKE IT!

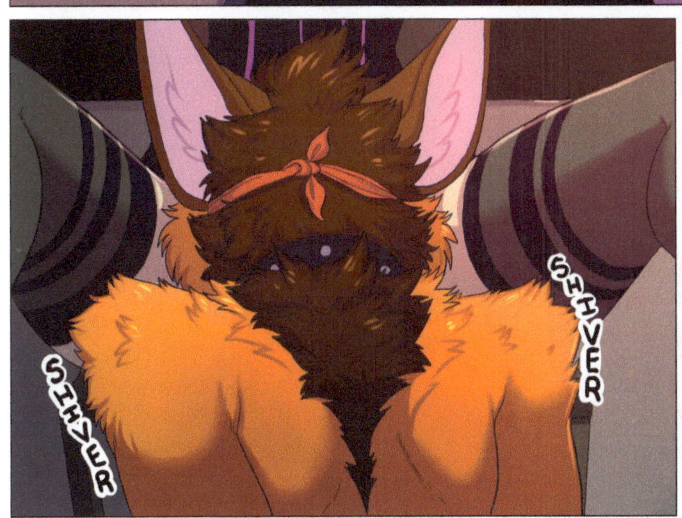

SHIVER
SHIVER

♥WHINE

HOLD IT.
NNH

STAY.
MMFF

OK.
GUH
DROP IT!

GASP

ARE YOU ALRIGHT?
DO YOU WANT TO SLOW DOWN?
I'M...
GREAT!
PANT
PANT

BUT REALLY

IS THAT ALL YOU GOT?

OH!
YOU KNOW IT'S NOT.
WE'RE JUST GETTING STARTED.

YOU'VE BEEN GOOD SO FAR.
-SO I CAN GET TO WORK.
OH.
HOW ABOUT YOU TURN THAT CUTE BUTT AROUND-

UM-
ABOUT THAT.

...
IS IT OK IF WE USE THE 'OTHER THING'?
I DON'T WANT TO GET TOO BEAT UP TODAY.

HMM. GOOD POINT.

LET'S SEE...
I THINK I HAVE A SOLUTION.

OPEN UP.
AH

WIDER!
AH- GULK!

THERE.
IF YOU DON'T WANT TO GO HARD I CAN THINK OF SOMETHING MUCH SOFTER TO DO.
YESH SUUH.

NICE!
THICK.
WARM.
EXACTLY WHAT I'M LOOKING FOR.
ISH IT?
YES. IT'S PERFECT.
THANK YOU.
THIS IS FAMILIAR TERRAIN.
YOU SHOULDN'T HAVE ANY PROBLEMS.
DON'T BE SHY.
START LICKING, MUTT.

MMMH
GET IN THERE!
S.LURP.
AH
THAT'S IT.
LICK
DEEPER BOY!
MPHH
SLIDE

YES-
AH!

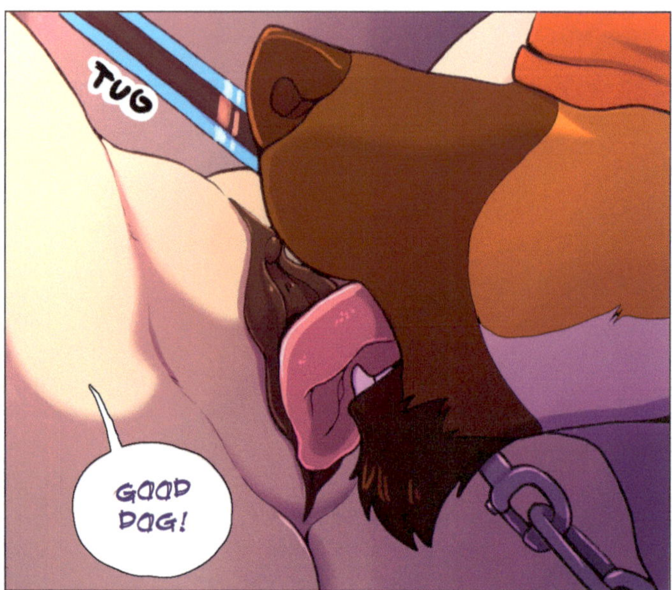

TUG
GOOD DOG!

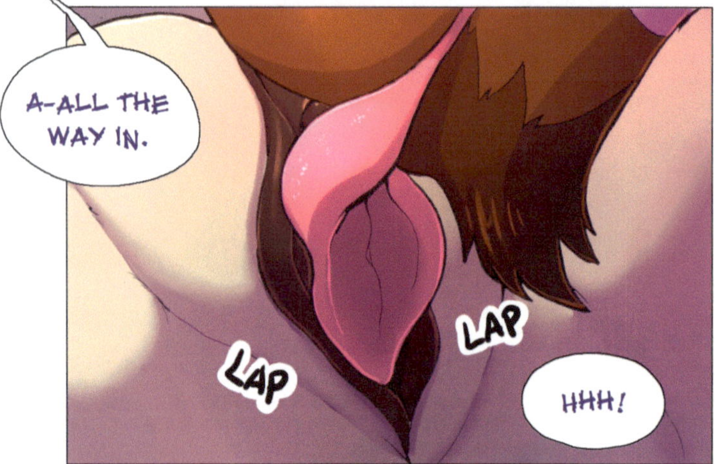

A-ALL THE WAY IN.
LAP
LAP
HHH!

HHN!
RIGHT THERE!
PRESS

THAT'S THE SPOT!
SLURP

SQUISH
OOOH!

AH!
SUCK
SHHH
SUCK
R-RIGHT THERE.
FUCK!
KEEP IT UP.
DON'T-
-STOP!
SQUEEZE
AH!
O-OH!
YES!
I'M GONNA-
HUFF
HUFF
HUFF
AHN
I'M GONNA-

AAH GOD DAMNIT!
FUCK.
WAG
WAG
WAG

GOOD SHIT.
SNRT
WAH!
YOM
OK! OK.
YOU DID GOOD.
SWRP
CALM DOWN.

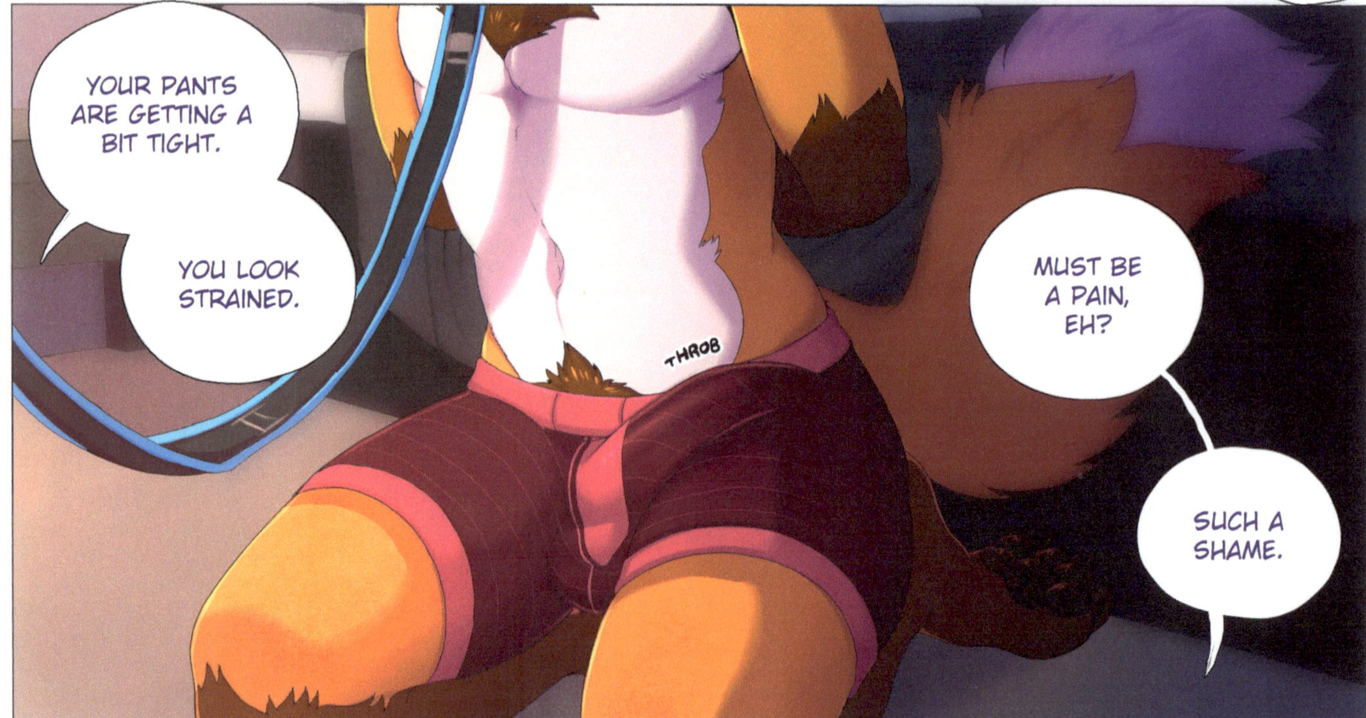

YOUR PANTS ARE GETTING A BIT TIGHT.
YOU LOOK STRAINED.
THROB
MUST BE A PAIN, EH?
SUCH A SHAME.

SUCH A BAD BOY!
GETTING RANDY AND WET OVER FAN-SERVICE.
YEAH?!
I GOT YOU MORE THAN JUST WET-
WHAT WAS THAT?
UH-UH!
TALKING BACK?
NOW IS NOT THE TIME TO GET SASSY, BUD.
IN FACT, I THINK IT'S TIME WE MOVE TO THE BED.
THE BED?
I HAVE A BLINDFOLD ON!
YOU'RE LEANING ON IT RIGHT NOW.
USE YOUR LEGS.

THERE WE GO, SEE?
THAT WASN'T SO HARD.
THOUGH-

I CAN'T SAY THE SAME FOR THE REST OF YOU.

THESE WERE GOING AWAY-

AT ONE POINT OR ANOTHER!
BETTER?
MUCH.
NOW-

TURN AROUND!
LET ME SEE THAT CUTE TOOSH!

NICE.
10/10
HOLD ON.
I NEED TO GET SOME THINGS.

LET'S SEE!

THERE ARE A LOT OF INTERESTING THINGS IN HERE!

YOU REALLY DID GO ALL OUT!
I BET THE FOLKS AT THAT SHOP LOVED YOU.
HM! I THINK I FOUND JUST THE THING TOO!
SPLURT
BUT FIRST.
LET ME LOOSEN YOU UP A BIT.

LET ME SEE THAT REAR.
TAIL UP.
GRAB
WIGGLE
WIGGLE
DRIP
IT'S BEEN A LONG TIME-
SQUISH
-SINCE I'VE BEEN BACK HERE.
SQUEEZE
YOU'VE GOTTEN EASIER.
RUB
RUB
HAVE YOU BEEN PRACTICING? WITHOUT ME?
SLCH
SLCH
NH.. NGH.
N-NO...
LIAR!
BAD DOG!
BOYS WHO TELL LIES-
-NEED TO BE PUNISHED.
AH... YES...

YOU AGREE THEN!
AW
I CAN'T SAY NO TO THAT BUTT.
JUST FOR THAT-

I'LL FULFILL YOUR EARLIER REQUEST!
SHING

AH!
DRIP
BREATHE.
NHHN.

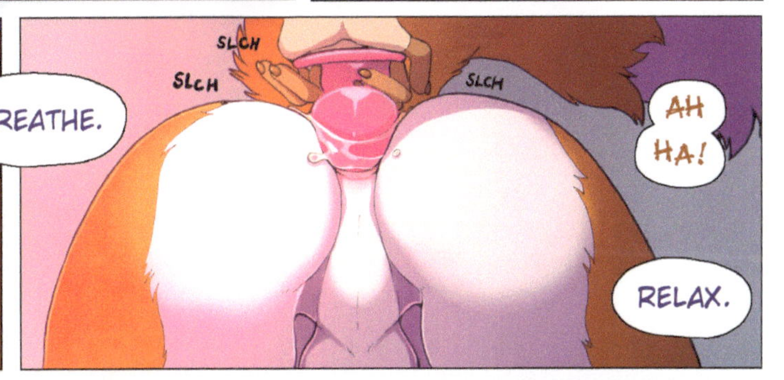

SLCH
SLCH
SLCH
AH HA!
RELAX.

POP!
HERE!
SLIPS RIGHT IN, DOESN'T IT?
GOOD BOY.
GRRR
NO GROWLING!

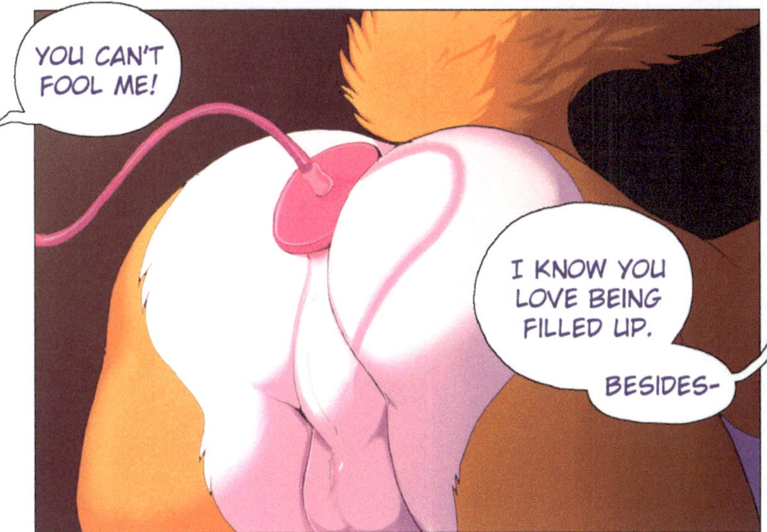

YOU CAN'T FOOL ME!
I KNOW YOU LOVE BEING FILLED UP.
BESIDES-

-YOUR PUNISHMENT-
SQUEEZE
- HAS JUST BEGUN!

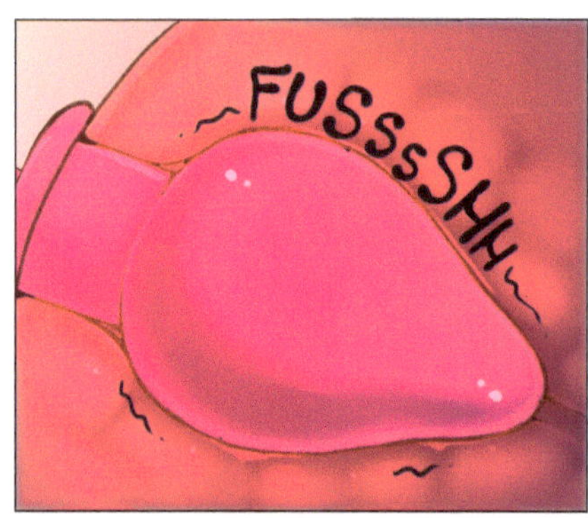
FUSSsSHH

GUH?!

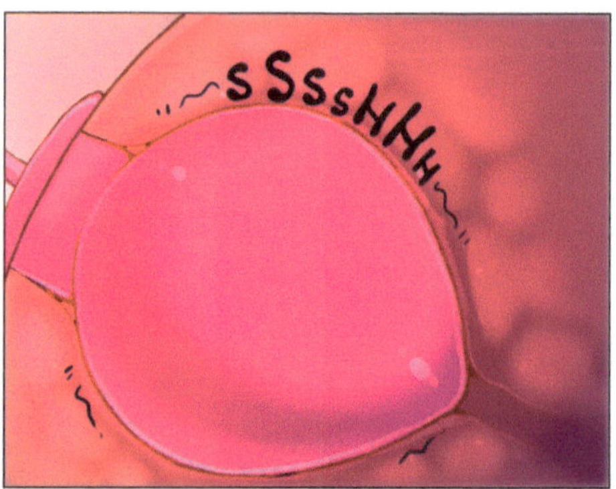
SSSSHHH

NGH!
JUST A FEW PUMPS.
NICE AND TIGHT.
HM...
F-FUCK.

CLICK
WONDER WHAT THIS DOES.
OH!
LOVELY!
TUG
GURK!
VVRRR RRRr
NOW, COME HERE-
WHIRRRr

S-
COUGH
COUGH

SP...
SORRY!
WHEEZE

TOO MUCH?
A LITTLE BIT.
PANT

IT'S OK!
I JUST NEED A BREAK-
-TO CATCH MY BREATH.
KISS

OK! LET ME KNOW IF YOU'RE GOOD TO KEEP GOING.
I'M FINE.
TO BE HONEST, WITH THIS INSIDE ME IT'S AWKWARD SITTING.
I'D RATHER NOT DESTROY YOUR NECK-
-YET.
AND LOUD WITHOUT YOU TALKING OVER IT.

OH? SO YOU WANT TO KEEP GOING?
TCH! BACK ON THE BED PUPPER.
YUP! AND UH- YOU CAN STILL TUG ON ME IF YOU WANT.
LET'S PLAY.
YESSIR!

FLIP OVER.
I DON'T HAVE MUCH USE FOR YOUR BACK ANYMORE.
GOOD DOG.
NOW GET COMFY.
YOU ONLY HAVE ONE VERY IMPORTANT INSTRUCTION FROM NOW ON.
AND WHAT'S THAT?
WH-WHAT?! THAT'S MEAN!
YOU'RE NOT ALLOWED TO CUM-
-UNLESS I SAY SO.
TOO BAD!
VVVRRR

HONK!
SQUEEZE
SQUEEZE
DON'T-
DON'T DO THAT.
SORRY. THAT DOESN'T COUNT.
TUG
OH. G-GOOD.
YOU CAN'T JUST TELL ME NOT TO FINISH.
IT'S TOO HARD WHEN YOU KEEP TOUCHING ME.
THAT'S THE POINT.
YOU SHOULD LEARN A LITTLE SELF CONTROL.
NO MATTER WHAT'S HAPPENING.
HUFF HUFF HU
ESPECIALLY IF IT FEELS GOOD.
GOOD DOGS FOLLOW COMMANDS.
WITHOUT QUESTION.
RELAX.
I'LL BE GENTLE.
DRIP
FUCK.

SO MUCH TENSION.
LET'S EASE THAT OUT.
NH!
THIS MUST BE TORTUROUS FOR YOU
HUH?
BUT NOT ALL TORTURE HAS TO BE BAD.
HERE.
LET'S SLIP YOU INTO SOMETHING MORE-
Ahh... HA...
-COMFORTABLE.
NNH
WHAT-
WHAT IS THAT!

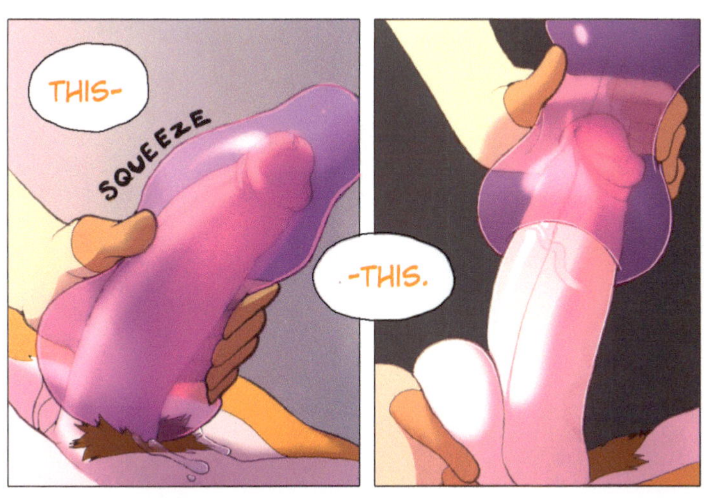

THIS-
SQUEEZE
-THIS.

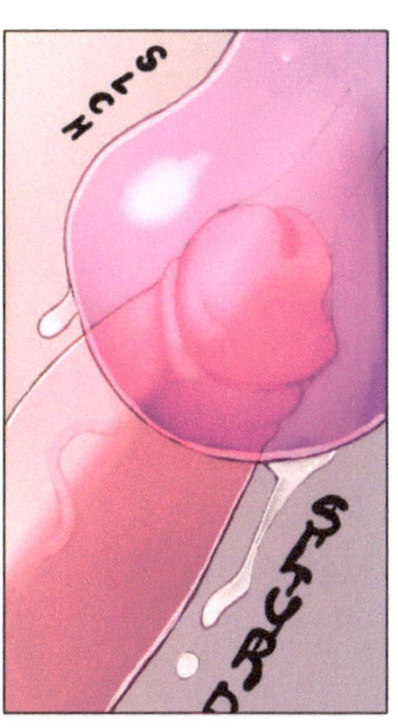

ISN'T FAIR!
NNGH

SORRY PAL!
I CAN'T HEAR YOU OVER THIS LOUD BUZZING!

A-AH...

YOU'RE NOT
PLAYING FAIR!
THROB
THROB
NOT FAIR?

ALL'S FAIR IN LOVE AND WAR.
BUT-

YOU CAN ALWAYS TELL ME TO STOP.
IF YOU DON'T LIKE IT.

NEVER.
THAT'S MY BOY!
YOU'RE TAKING THIS WELL.
I'M IMPRESSED.
YOU KNOW-
THERE'S ANOTHER PLACE WE CAN PUT THIS.
WARMER
WETTER...
TIGHTER.
BUT BEFORE WE DO THAT.
I WANT YOU-
-TO BEG FOR IT.

MMM
NOW.
TELL ME YOU WANT ME.
I WANT YOU.
NOPE!
TRY AGAIN.
NGH! SANDRA!
OH, PLEASE! YOU DON'T MEAN IT. NOT YET.
THROB
I WANT TO HEAR YOUR VOICE CRACK.

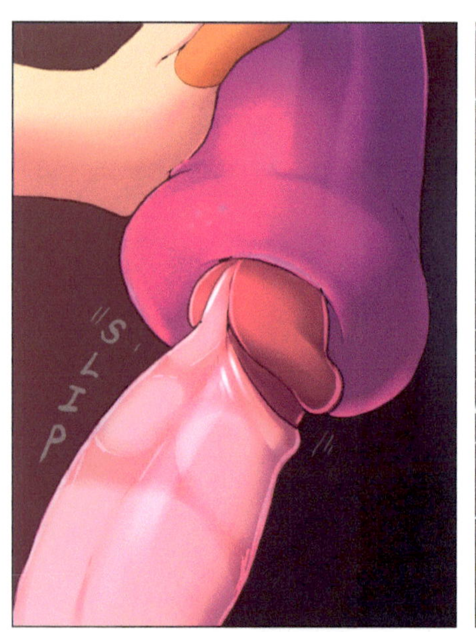

SLIP

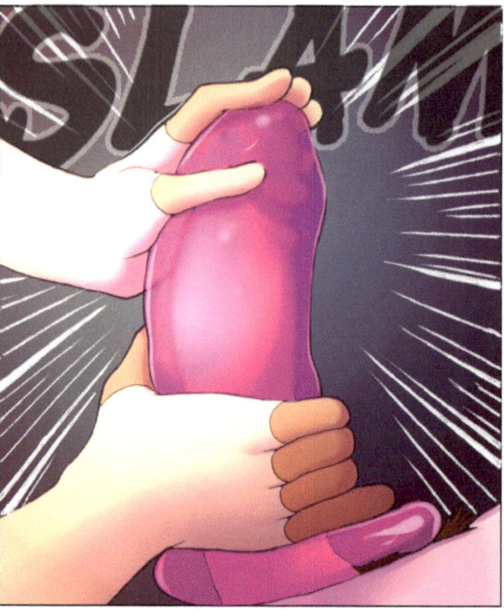

SLAM
POP!

YIKES!

I DIDN'T EXPECT IT TO GO THROUGH.
YOUR SIZE IS KIND OF A PAIN IN THE ASS.
BUT-
SLCH
NOM
YOU LIKE WHEN GIRLS TELL YOU THAT-
HUH?

YOU'VE BEEN HOLDING YOUR TONGUE.
FOR ONCE
MAYBE YOU'RE READY TO TRY AGAIN?
I-
WON'T BEG.
SUIT YOURSELF.
BUT SOMETHING TELLS ME-
-YOU'RE NOT GOING TO LAST MUCH LONGER.
I CAN FEEL YOU SQUIRMING.
ACHING.
I-IT'S THE VIBRATOR.
GASP
OH. I'M SURE IT IS.

YOU'RE BLUFFING, AND I'LL PROVE IT.
YOU FORGET. I HAVE LEVERAGE.
BOTTOMS UP!
SHIT, OK I HAVEN'T DONE THIS IN A WHILE.
HE CAN'T SEE YOU.
GUH!
DEEP BREATH.
AH!
SLOWLY.
NGH!
ALL THE WAY DOWN. F-FUCK... HE'S HUGE.
HOLD STILL BIG GUY.
DON'T YOU DARE THRUST.
MMMPH!
G-GAH!

COME ON!
THERE'S NO WAY YOU CAN STAND THIS.
NH!
THIS IS WORKING, RIGHT?
MPH
YEP
STILL BUZZIN'
GUH
SHIT.
HOLDING OUT IS HOT AND ALL
BUT-
WAIT! HE'S NOT GONNA CUM IN HERE IS HE?!
I STILL NEED HIM TO-
SHUDDER
NNN FUCK IT!
I CAN'T!
PLEASE!

PLEASE!
FOR FUCKS SAKE!
BINGO.
AGH!

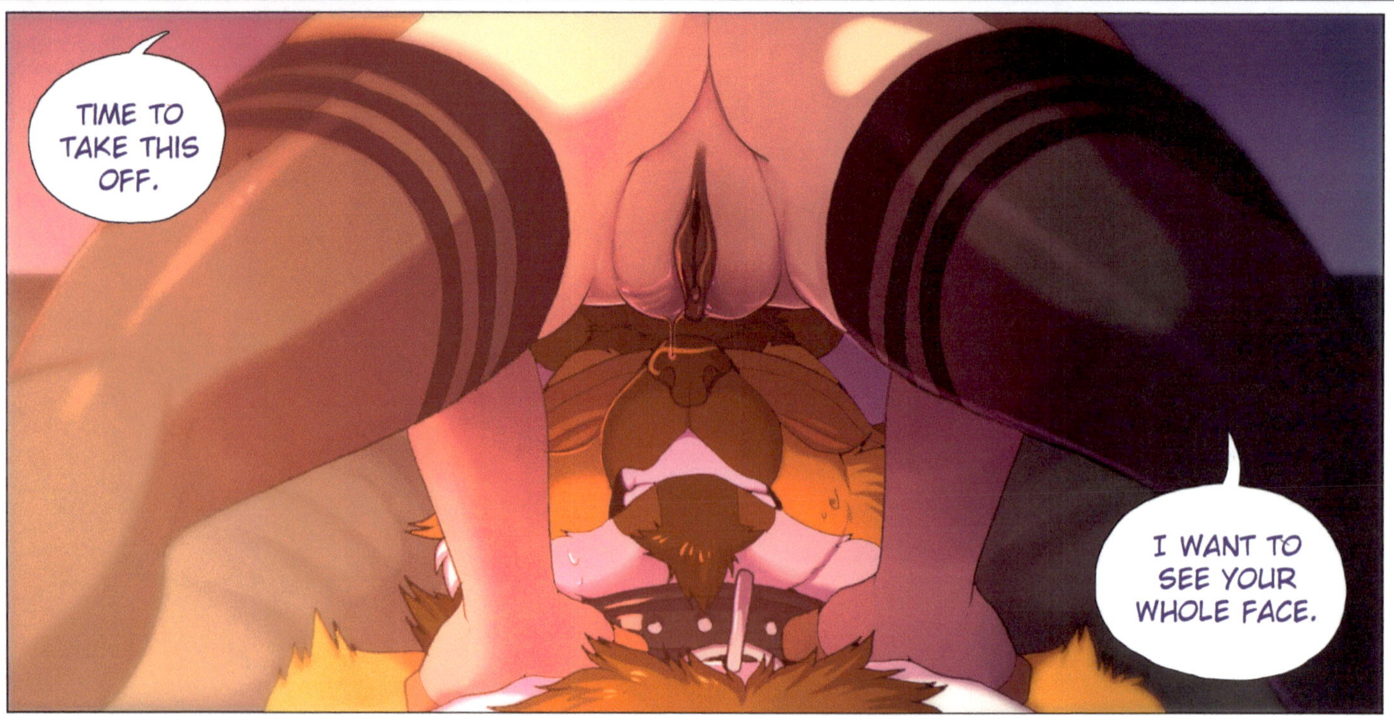

LOOK AT YOU.
SO SQUIRMY.
THAT WASN'T EVEN THE REAL THING.
BUT SINCE YOU FINALLY ASKED NICELY
I'LL REWARD YOU.
TIME TO TAKE THIS OFF.
I WANT TO SEE YOUR WHOLE FACE.

THERE WE GO!
I ALMOST FORGOT HOW BEAUTIFUL YOUR EYES ARE.
RIGHT BACK AT YAH.
I MISSED YOU TOO.
AH MAN...
YOU'RE SUCH A MUSH PUDDLE RIGHT NOW.
IT MUST BE THAT THING IN YOUR ASS.
IT'S MAKING NICE VIBRATIONS, AT LEAST.

WET
WARM
YOU WANT THIS?
HUH.
YOU KNOW
I MIGHT HAVE MORE STAMINA RIGHT NOW.
PATHETIC
I WAS HOPING FOR A CHALLENGE.
DON'T LET ME DOWN.
OH WELL.
LET'S SEE HOW LONG YOU CAN HOLD OUT.
NEVER.

IT'S BEEN A WHILE.
YOU'RE MAKING MY CORSET WORK.
THAT'S IT.
I CAN FEEL YOU TWITCHING.
GET ALL THE WAY IN.
I LIKE MY BOYS DEEP.

I'LL MAKE SURE TO FUCK YOU UNTIL YOU CAN'T STAND-

AH!
FUCK!
THRUST

OH.

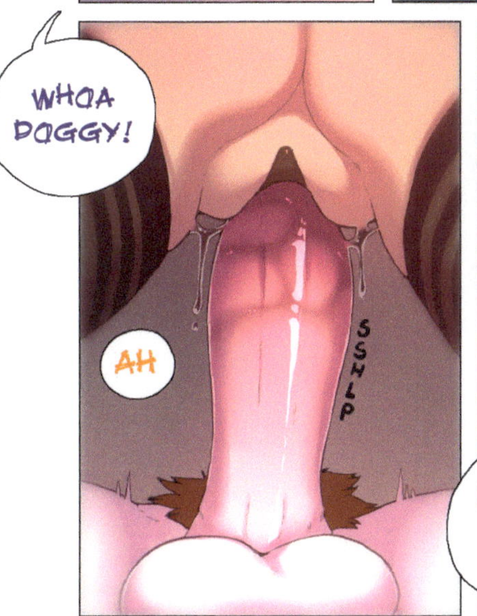

WHOA DOGGY!
AH
SSHLP

LOOKS LIKE SOMEONE FLIPPED
YOUR 'ON' SWITCH.
SLUP
FFPH
AHH

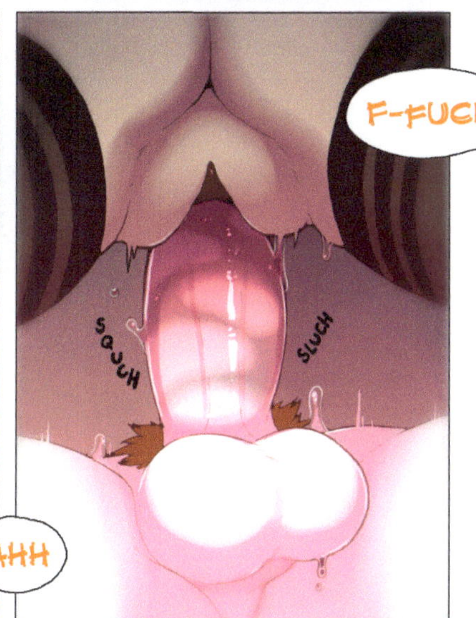

F-FUCK
SQUCH
SLUCH

GOOD BOY
BUCK INTO ME.
FILL ME UP.
I REALLY HAH NEED TO...
SANDRA
I'M GONNA CUM.
NOT YET.
JUST CONCENTRATE ON ME.
AND KEEP WHIMPERING, MUTT.
I WANT TO HEAR YOU.
P-PLEASE!
AH... NNH
THROB
THAT'S IT, ALMOST THERE.
CLENCH

HERE WE GO.
GET NICE AND DEEP.
GOOD DOG.
SHURP
ARE YOU READY, MUTT?
NNNH
YOU'RE GONNA CUM HARD FOR ME IN
THREE...
TWO..
ONE.

AH!
CUM
NNNH!
SPLURT
BITE
FUUUCKK
BLRP
MMMPPH!
BLRP
BLP
MMMFF
MMRR

OH
MY
GOD

OOH
MY
GOOOD
HMM

GOOD BOY.
COME ON.
LET'S GET YOU OUT OF THOSE CUFFS.
YOU'VE HAD ENOUGH OF BEING TIED UP FOR ONE NIGHT.
THAT'S WHERE IT WAS?!

FOR BEING SO FLUFFY THOSE GET SORE AFTER A BIT.
I SHOULD HAVE INVESTED IN THE COMFIER ONES.

HEY
HOW ABOUT WE ALSO GET THIS THING OUT?
...TAKE IT OUT?
YOU KNOW...

YOU AREN'T DONE, RIGHT?
PRECIOUS BOY.

UUUH?

DUDE.
I...

JUST CAME...
THAT'S NICE.

I DIDN'T.
SO I WANT YOU TO FUCK ME UNTIL I DO.

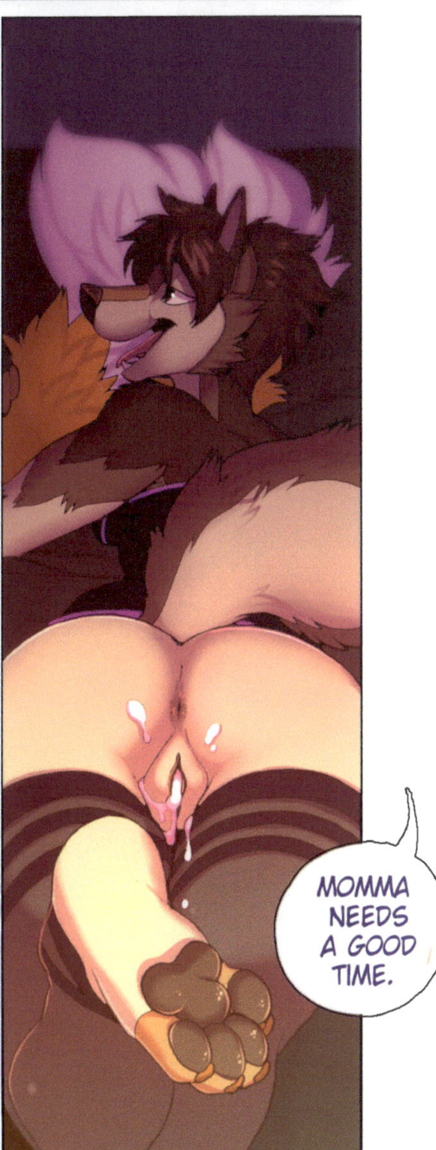

IT SHOULD BE EASY, WITH THE MESS YOU MADE.
YEAH, THAT'S THE PROBLEM.
REFRACTORY PERIOD N' ALL.
YOU HAVE OTHER BODY PARTS.
10 OF THEM TO BE PRECISE.
MOMMA NEEDS A GOOD TIME.

OK
OK.

UH-
GIVE ME A SECOND HERE.

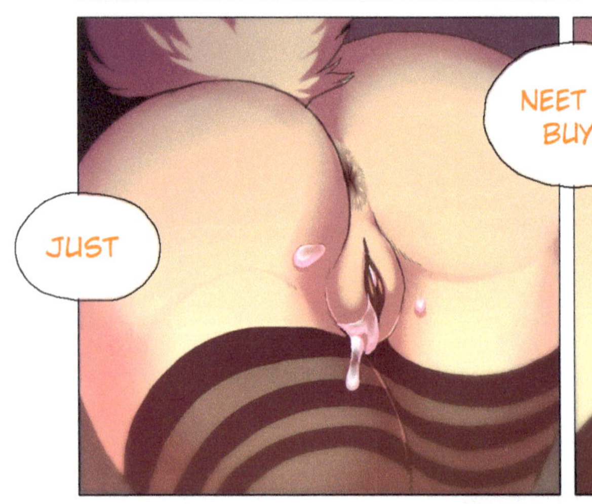

JUST

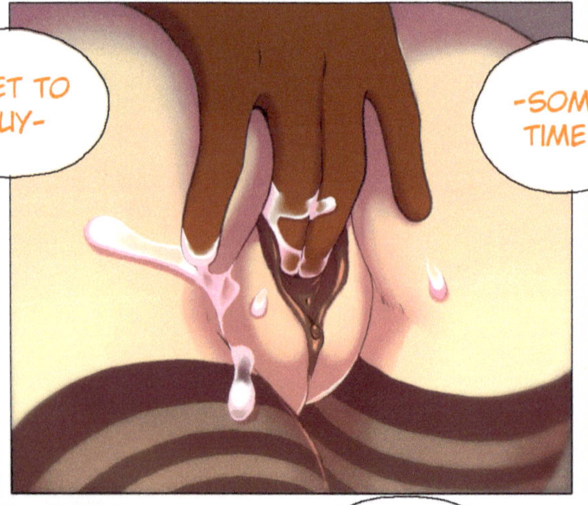

NEET TO BUY-

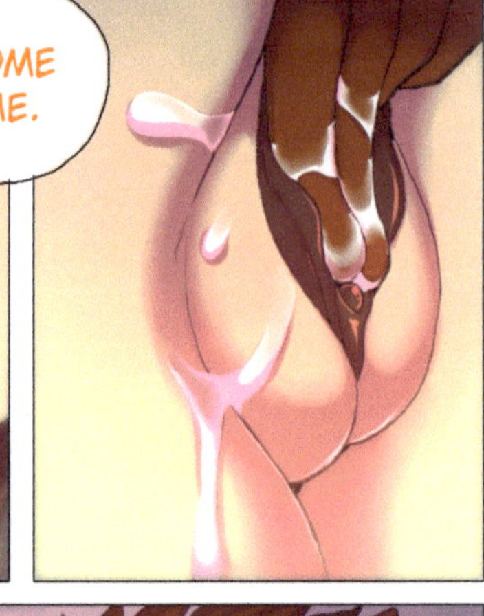

-SOME TIME.

MMMH
NOM
BUY ALL THE TIME YOU NEED.

OK

BUT

I NEED A NEW ANGLE.

OOOH!
THAT WAS FAST.
NOT QUITE THERE YET, BUT THIS IS HELPING.
HAHA, DON'T CALL MY BUTT THAT!

MMHM
NICE MOOSHY CUSHIONS!
WHAT-

YOU'VE CALLING ME THINGS ALL NIGHT.
IT'S ONLY FAIR.
SHH
LESS TEASING, MORE PLEASING.

YOU'RE LUCKY YOU MAKE ME SO HARD.
OH YEAH?
PROVE IT!

AS YOU WISH, SIR.
PUT IT IN M'LADY.

OH FUCK YOU—MMH

UHN!
HAH

AH!
GOOD BOY!

LET'S SEE ...
CAN WE MAKE THIS EVEN MORE EXCITING?
TODAY IS A DAY OF LEARNING.
MAYBE, A LITTLE MORE EXPERIMENTATION IS NEEDED.

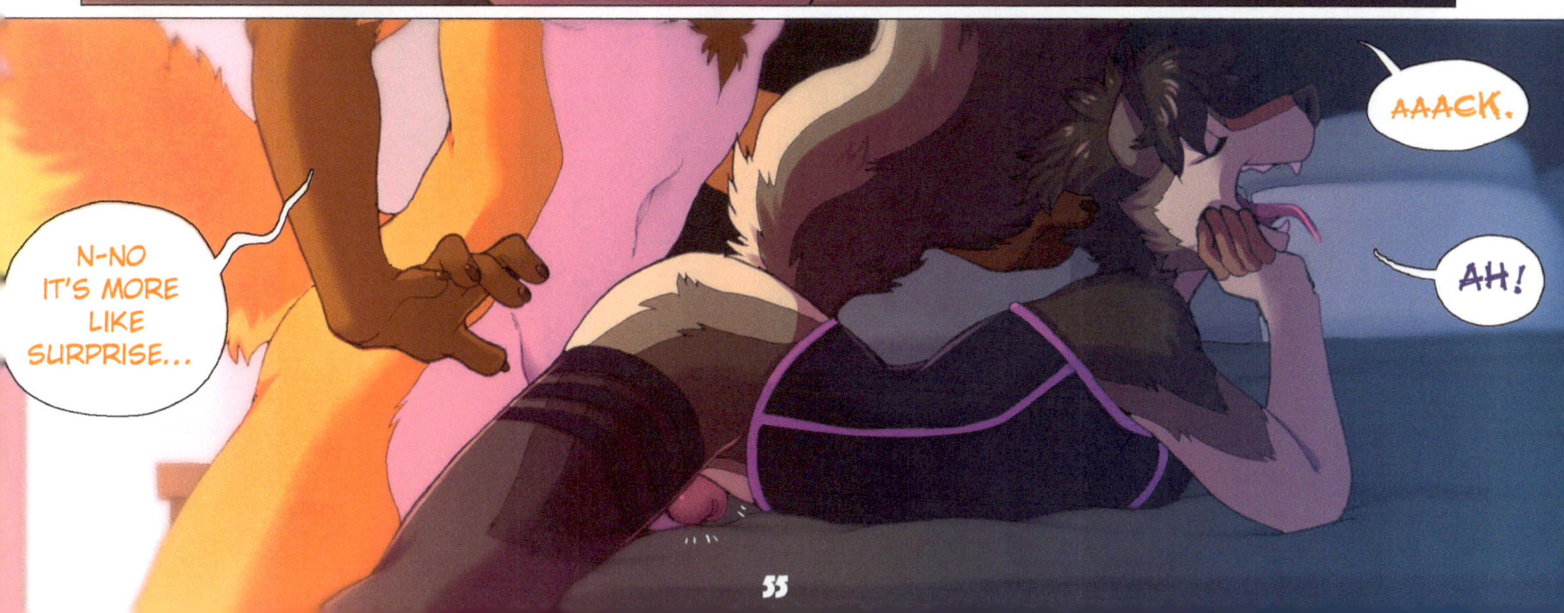

WHAT THE FUCK???
BZZ~ZZT
OOPS SORRY.
THIS THING ONLY HAS TWO SETTINGS
WHAT?
GENTLE AND JACKHAMMER?
HOLY SSHHIT!
BRZ~ZZ
HAHA I CAN ACTUALLY FEEL IT THROUGH YOUR DICK.
THAT'S KINDA GOOFY.
SLORP
WHOOPS.
OOOH YEAH, THAT'S A NICE PLACE FOR IT.
GOOD IDEA.
N-NO IT'S MORE LIKE SURPRISE...
AAACK.
AH!

F-FUCK
OH YES.
CHOKE ME DADDY.

NGH...
OK.
LET'S DO THIS.
HELL YEAH.

SH-SHIT.
GET UP IN THERE.
UHN
AND GO AS SLOW AS YOU WANT.

MMMH.
BZZZZT

FUCK
YOU'RE SO SOFT.
MMHM
TELL ME MORE.
UNGH
BUT I'D PROBABLY FINISH AGAIN TOO SOON.
WOULDN'T THAT BE A SH-SHAME!
THRUST
I COULD
DID YOUR VOICE ACTUALLY QUIVER?
WHAT'S THAT?
IT'S THE VIBRATOR...
A-AH!
OF COURSE.

HEY
I REALLY WANT TO SEE YOUR FACE.
DO YOU MIND IF WE TURN AROUND?
OH?
HOW'S THIS.
PERFECT.
AH...
FUCK.
MMPH!
THAT'S A GOOD BOY.
SO CUTE.

SPLORT!
SPLURP!
SPLORTP!
SHIT, THAT MAKES A GOOFY NOISE.
UHN GEEZE.

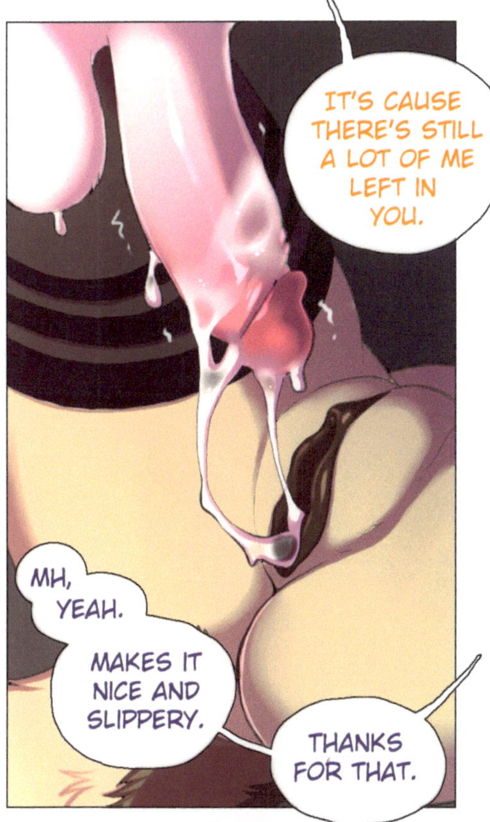

IT'S CAUSE THERE'S STILL A LOT OF ME LEFT IN YOU.
MH, YEAH.
MAKES IT NICE AND SLIPPERY.
THANKS FOR THAT.

OK
SOMETHING LESS NOISY THEN?
AHN!
YOU'RE BEING SUCH A TEASE!
HA HA

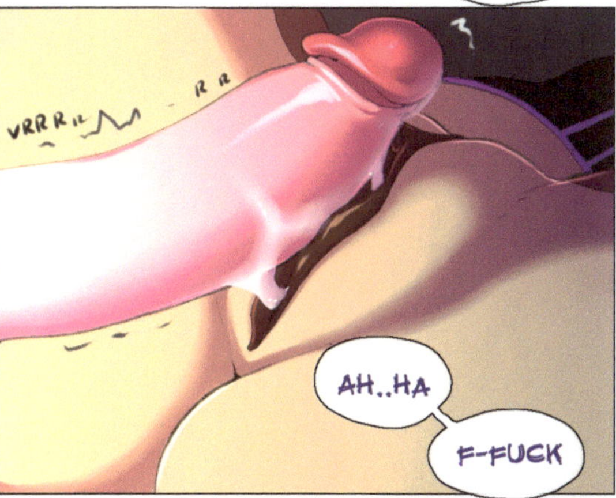

VRRR RR
AH..HA
F-FUCK

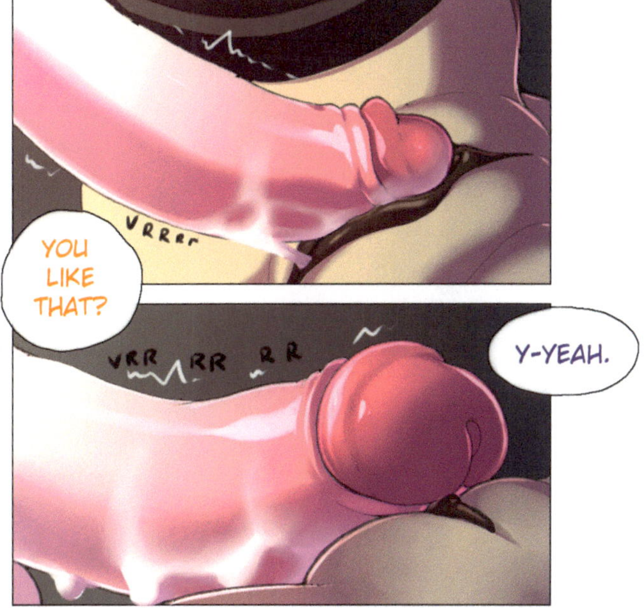

VRRR
YOU LIKE THAT?
VRR RR RR
Y-YEAH.

FUCK DUDE!
AH!
NH... SHIT.
H-HOW ARE YOU?
I'M GETTING THERE.
COME HERE YOU.
MMMH!
GOOD BOY.
I THINK I'M READY FOR YOU TO GO BACK IN.
YOU SURE?
ABSOLUTELY.
YES, SIR.
BUT DO IT FAST.

OOH!
OH YEAH.
THAT'S THE SPOT!
RIGHT THERE...
I'M CLOSE BUT-
A-AHN!
HA HA
IT LOOKS LIKE YOU'RE ALREADY THERE.
GRUNT

AH FUCK!
WHAT ABOUT YOU?

NHH!
F-FUUCK!
AH!
HA HA WOW!
PANT
PANT
PANT

I'M SURPRISED YOU HAD THAT MUCH LEFT ON ROUND TWO.
YOU FILLED ME UP GOOD BEN.
WELL
YOU GET ME GOING PRETTY HARD.

YOU'RE SO BEAUTIFUL.
AW

I LOVE YOU.

OK!
GET OFF ME, BEN.
YOU'RE A HEAVY BOY.

WAS IT GOOD FOR YOU TOO?
YESSS.
THANKS FOR HUMORING ME, BY THE WAY.
OH?
WAS THAT WHAT IT WAS?
AREN'T YOU JUST FILLED TO THE BRIM WITH CHARM.
AT LEAST I'M NOT FILLED TO THE TAINT WITH JIZZ.

OH.. HA HA!
EITHER WAY, I'M GLAD YOU LIKED IT.
I HAD FUN.

MAYBE NEXT TIME
WE CAN GET MORE ROWDY.
MORE?
YEAH!

WE CAN BUY BETTER CUFFS, A GAG, MAYBE A SWING?
I THINK THERE ARE LOAD BEARING BEAMS IN HERE SOMEWHERE.
HOW DO YOU FEEL ABOUT SPANKING?
HEY, HEY.
COME HERE.

HOW ABOUT WE ORDER IN AND TAKE A BREAK?
SURE
LET ME TURN THIS OFF.

IN THE MEANTIME IT SEEMS WE NEED TO DO LAUNDRY.
A BIG LOAD TOO

SOMETHING YOU CAN DO, HUN!
YOU'RE NOT TOO TIRED... RIGHT?
W-WAIT...!

NO. THAT WASN'T PART OF THE PLAN!
I JUST WANT TO CUDDLE ON THE COUCH.

SORRY!
CAN'T HEAR YOU OVER THE SOUND OF ALL THE PEPPERONI PIZZA!
YOU BETTER TAKE THAT PLUG OUT

BEFORE THE DELIVERY GUY GETS HERE.
MMMHH...

I STILL CAN'T BELIEVE YOU'VE NEVER BEEN HANDCUFFED BEFORE.
UNTIL I MET YOU MOST OF MY PARTNERS PREFERED BOTTOMING.
I DON'T MIND THE WORK, BUT WITH YOU IT'S DIFFERENT.
THANKS FOR BEING COMFORTABLE TRYING NEW THINGS WITH ME.
I LOVE YOU.
THERE'S NO ONE I'D RATHER TRY THINGS WITH THAN YOU.
YEAH?
YOU'RE A WORKOUT THOUGH. I'M READY TO PASS OUT.
AW. ONLY IF YOU DO IT ON ME.
ALWAYS.
END

BEN

MANED WOLF

SANDRA
TIMBER WOLF

SPECIAL THANKS TO THE SUPPORTERS
ON PATREON FOR PROVIDING THE MEANS
FOR ME TO KEEP DOING WHAT I LOVE

AND

TO YOU, THE READER

WITHOUT YOU, THIS COMIC WOULD NOT BE
POSSIBLE.

THANK YOU SO MUCH!

ARTIST BIO

HELLO!

I'M ACE, AN ARTIST. I SPEND MOST OF MY TIME WORKING OUT OF THE
WEST COAST OF SUNNY CALIFORNIA. I'VE ALWAYS ENJOYED DRAWING
SINCE I WAS IN HIGH SCHOOL AND IT'S SOMETHING I'VE BEEN
WORKING HARD ON FOR A LONG TIME. I REALLY ENJOY DRAWING FOR
THE FURRY FANDOM AND I HOPE MY WORK CAN MAKE SOMEONE'S DAY
MORE ENJOYABLE.

WHETHER YOU'VE PURCHASED THIS COMIC OR RECEIVED IT AS A GIFT,
I'D LIKE TO THANK YOU FOR YOUR SUPPORT AND HOPE THAT YOU
ENJOY THIS COMIC AND MY OTHER WORKS.

YOU CAN FIND MORE OF MY ART AT
WWW.FURAFFINITY.NET/USER/ROANOAK

MY PATREON (FOR MORE COMIC FUN)
WWW.PATREON.COM/PEPPERMINTHUSKY

YOU CAN ALSO FIND MY WORK ON TWITTER
WWW.TWITTER.COM/AYCEEART